My Adventures with the Velveteen Rabbit

This book
was
especially written
for
Jenna Marie Chiavelli
with love
from
Aunt Anna Marie

Written by Margaret Gibson
Illustrated by Ester Kasepuu

There was once a Velveteen Rabbit, and in the beginning he was really splendid. He was plump and cuddly, as a rabbit should be; his coat was spotted brown and white, he had real thread whiskers, and his ears were lined with pink satin.

On Christmas morning he sat wedged in the top of Jenna Marie Chiavelli's stocking, with a sprig of holly between his paws.

There were other things in the stocking but the Rabbit was the best of all. For at least two hours Jenna Marie played with him, and then lots of visitors came and there was a great unwrapping of presents. In all the excitement the Velveteen Rabbit was forgotten.

For a long time he lived in the toy cupboard at 10 Thomas Court, Woodcliff Lake, and no one thought much about him. The little Rabbit thought the other more expensive toys were all stuffed with sawdust like himself. But they teased the Velveteen Rabbit and said he was not Real. The only person who was kind to him was the Skin Horse.

Now Skin Horse had lived longer in the house than any of the others. Jenna Marie had a ride on him every day and when Joey, John and Jake came to play, they rode on Skin Horse as well. He had seen many mechanical toys who thought they were the best toys in the world, only to have their springs break and become useless. Toyland magic is wonderful, only those playthings that are old and wise like Skin Horse understand all about it.

'Does REAL mean having things that buzz inside you and wheels and things?' asked the Rabbit one day.

'Real isn't how you are made,' said Skin Horse. 'When a child loves you for a long, long time, not just to play with, but REALLY loves you, then you become REAL.'

'Does it happen all at once, like being wound up,' the Rabbit asked, 'or bit by bit?'

'It takes a long time,' said Skin Horse. 'By the time you are Real, most of your hair has been loved off and your eye buttons have dropped out and you are very shabby.' Skin Horse rocked backwards and forwards. 'But these things don't matter. Once you are Real you can't be ugly, except to people who don't understand.'

'Are you Real?' said the Rabbit.
Skin Horse smiled. 'Long ago a child loved me and this made me Real. Once you become Real it lasts for always.'
The Rabbit sighed. He longed to become Real, and yet the idea of becoming shabby and losing his eye buttons and whiskers was rather sad.

One evening, when Jenna Marie was going to bed, she looked in the toy cupboard.

'Oh, here is my bunny,' she whispered to herself. That night, and for many nights after, the Velveteen Rabbit slept in Jenna Marie's bed. He soon grew to like it. Jenna Marie made nice tunnels for him under the bedclothes, that she said were like the burrows real rabbits lived in. When Jenna Marie dropped off to sleep, the Rabbit would snuggle down close and dream, with Jenna Marie's hands clasped close around him all night long.

Time went on. The little Rabbit was so happy that he never noticed how his beautiful velveteen fur was getting shabby, and his tail became unsewn, and all the pink rubbed off his nose where Jenna Marie had kissed him. Spring came, and Jenna Marie and the Velveteen Rabbit had long days in the garden, for wherever Jenna Marie went the Rabbit went too. He had rides in the wheelbarrow and picnics on the grass. And once, when Jenna Marie was called away suddenly for tea, the Rabbit was left outside until long after dusk. He was wet through with the dew and quite grubby from diving into the tunnels that Jenna Marie had made for him in the garden.

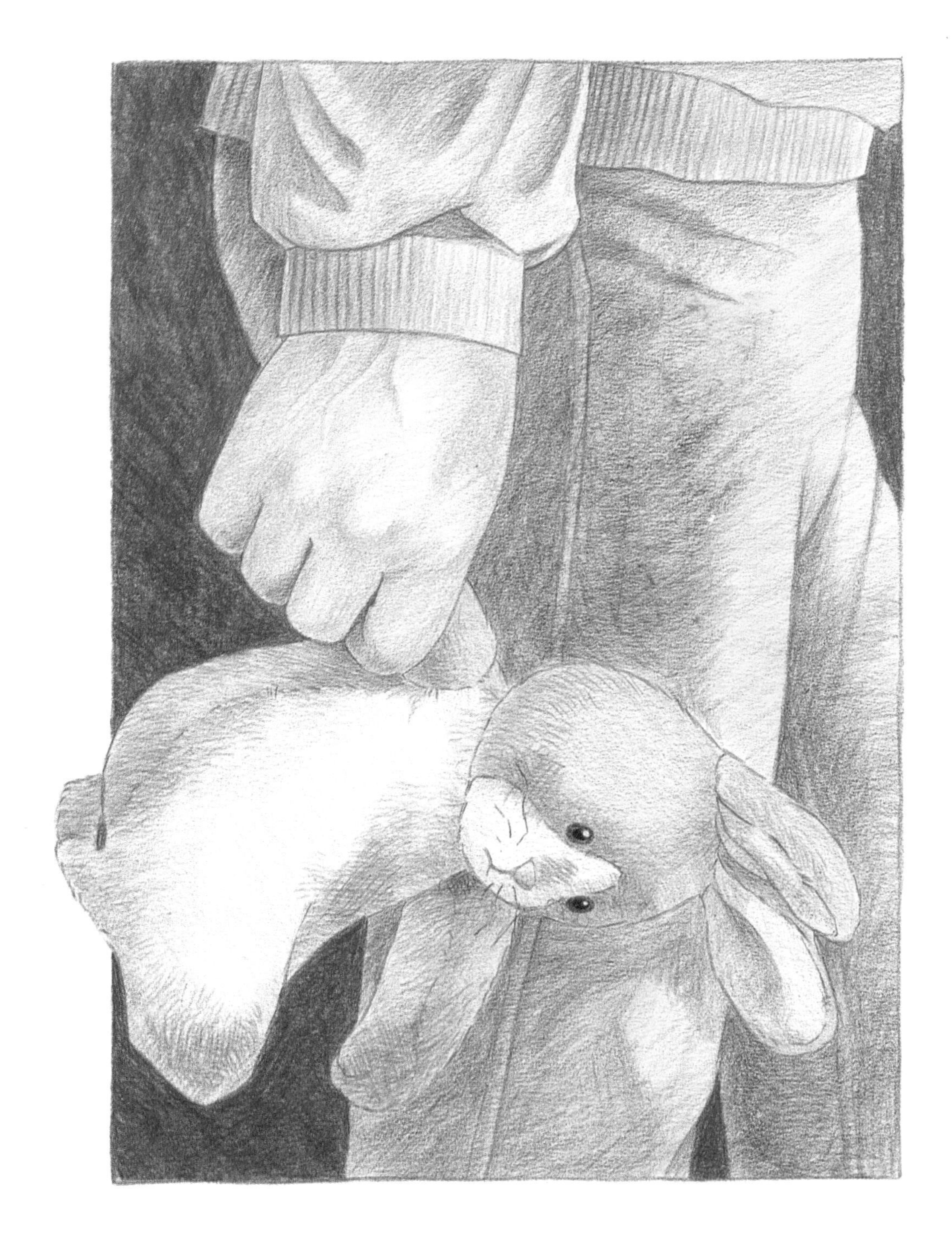

A Big Person picked him up, rubbed the dirt off him and took him back to Jenna Marie, grumbling, 'Fancy all that fuss for a toy!' Jenna Marie sat up in bed and stretched out her hands.

'Give me my Bunny!' she said. 'He isn't a toy. He's REAL!'

When the little Rabbit heard that, he was happy. He was Real. Jenna Marie herself had said it. He knew what Skin Horse had said was true at last. The magic had happened to him, and he was a toy no longer. That night he was almost too happy to sleep. So much love stirred in his little heart that it almost burst.

That was a wonderful Summer! Jenna Marie, Joey, John and Jake went to a holiday house near a big forest. Jenna Marie took the Velveteen Rabbit on long walks among the trees. She made little nests for him where he would be cosy while she played with her friends. Late one afternoon, while the Rabbit was lying there alone, he saw two strange things creep out of the tall grass near him. They were rabbits just like himself, but quite furry and brand-new.

They must have been very well made, for their seams didn't show at all, and they changed shape in a queer way when they moved instead of always staying the same like he did. They crept quite close to him. The Velveteen Rabbit stared hard to see where their clockwork winders stuck out on their backs. But he couldn't see any such thing. They must be a new kind of rabbit altogether.

'Why don't you get up and play with us?' one of them asked. But the Velveteen Rabbit didn't want to explain that he had no clockwork.

'Can you hop on your hind legs?' asked the furry rabbit. That was a dreadful question, for the Velveteen Rabbit had no hind legs at all! The back of him was made all in one piece. He hoped the other rabbits wouldn't notice.

But wild rabbits have very sharp eyes.

'Look, he hasn't got any hind legs!' laughed one of the rabbits.

'I have!' cried the little Velveteen Rabbit. 'I'm sitting on them!'

'Then stretch them out and show me, like this!' said the wild rabbit, beginning to whirl around and dance. The Velveteen Rabbit was longing, more than anything in the world, to be able to jump and dance. The wild rabbit stopped and came so close that his long whiskers brushed the Velveteen Rabbit's ears.

'Why, he isn't a rabbit at all!' he said, and jumped backwards. 'He isn't real!'

The little Velveteen Rabbit cried, 'I am Real! Jenna Marie said so!'

Just then Jenna Marie, Joey, John and Jake ran past them. With a stamp of their feet and a flash of white tails the two strange rabbits disappeared.

'Come back and play with me!' called the little Rabbit. 'I know I am Real.' But there was no answer. The Velveteen Rabbit was all alone. As the sun sank lower, Jenna Marie came and carried him home.

Weeks passed, and the little Rabbit grew very old and shabby, but Jenna Marie loved him just as much. She loved all his whiskers off. The pink lining in his ears turned gray and his coat faded. He scarcely looked like a rabbit any more, except to Jenna Marie. To her he was always beautiful.

One day, Jenna Marie was ill. Her face was flushed and she had to stay in bed. The little Velveteen Rabbit lay there hidden under the bedclothes. He thought of lots of lovely games to play when Jenna Marie got better and whispered special plans in her ear. Soon Jenna Marie was sitting up in bed looking at picture books, while the little Rabbit cuddled close at her side.
The day came when Jenna Marie was allowed out of bed. The little Rabbit lay among the bedclothes listening to Big People talking about vacation plans, for Jenna Marie was going away.

The Velveteen Rabbit
Margery Williams
The Velveteen Rabbit
M. Williams

He could hear a Big Person speaking:

'I think this is a good chance to sort out some of these old toys. Just look at this old Bunny! Time to throw him out! Today is the 13th of January, Jenna Marie's birthday, so we'll buy her a new bunny.'

And the little Rabbit was put in a bag, along with a lot of trash, and carried out to the end of the garden.

Later that day, Jenna Marie was given a splendid new white plush bunny. When she fell asleep that night she was too excited dreaming about her holiday to think about anything else.

The little Velveteen Rabbit lay among the trash and felt very lonely.

Happy Birthday

The bag had been left untied, and so by wriggling a bit he was able to get his head through the opening and look out. He could see the garden where he had played with Jenna Marie on sunlit mornings and a great sadness came over him. He remembered the wonderful day when Jenna Marie said he was Real.

Of what use was it to be loved and lose one's beauty and become Real, if it all ended like this? And a real tear trickled down his shabby velvet nose and fell to the ground.

And then a strange thing happened. Where the tear had fallen a beautiful flower grew out of the ground, so beautiful that the little Rabbit forgot to cry, and lay there watching it. The petals opened, and out of it stepped the loveliest fairy in the whole world. She gathered up the little Rabbit in her arms and kissed him on his soft nose.

'I am the Toyland Fairy,' she said, 'I take care of all the old and worn out playthings that children have loved. When they are not needed any more, I take them with me and make them Real.'

‘Wasn’t I Real before?’ asked the little Rabbit.

‘You were Real to Jenna Marie,’ the Fairy said, ‘because she loved you. Now you shall be Real to everyone.’

She held the little Rabbit close in her arms and flew into the forest. The moon had risen. In an open glade between the tree-trunks the wild rabbits danced. When they saw the Fairy they stopped and stood in a ring staring.

‘I’ve brought you a new playfellow,’ the Fairy said. ‘You must be kind to him and teach him all he needs to know in Rabbitland. He’s going to live with you for ever and ever.’

She kissed the little Rabbit again and put him down on the grass.

'Run and play, little Rabbit!' she said.

The little Rabbit sat very still. He didn't know that the last kiss had changed him altogether. Something tickled his nose, and he lifted his hind leg to scratch it. He had hind legs! They were no longer all in one piece! Instead of the dingy velveteen he now had soft brown fur. His ears twitched by themselves and his whiskers were so long they brushed the grass. He gave a leap of joy. He was a Real Rabbit at last, at home with the other rabbits!

The seasons passed and in the warm and sunny spring days Jenna Marie, Joey, John and Jake once more came to stay at the holiday house near the forest. While Jenna Marie was playing, two rabbits crept out from the long grass and looked at her. One of the rabbits had strange markings under his fur, as though long ago he had been spotted and the spots still showed through. Jenna Marie stood very still and looked at the little rabbit.

'Why,' she said, 'he looks just like my lovely old Bunny that was lost after I was ill.' But Jenna Marie never knew that it really was her own Velveteen Rabbit, come back to look at the child who had first helped him to be Real.